# PENSTRICKEN

Collected Stories

Andrew Ferguson

# CONTENTS

Title Page

Copyright

Christmas Eve                                    1

6 Six Word Stories (vol. 1)                     12

Popping Off                                      14

The Church Mouse                                 15

6 Six Word Stories (vol. 2)                      20

Little Thieves Are Hanged                        21

The Fireplace Coppers                            22

6 Six Word Stories (vol. 3)                      23

Santa: Origins                                   25

The Martian's Revenge                            29

6 Six Word Stories (vol. 4)                      31

The Secret of Sig. Pieroni's Pizza               33

I Need a Hero                                     35

6 Six Word Stories (vol. 5)                      40

Cold Brass                                       42

The Monster                              43
6 Six Word Stories (vol. 6)              44
The Girl & The Car                       46

# CHRISTMAS EVE

*First published 22nd December 2019*

K aren inhaled a sharp drag on her cigarette, holding the burning toxic fumes in her chest for as long as she could before letting them out in one shuddering breath on the snowy rooftops below.

It was freezing. Karen had sworn she'd never do another Christmas Eve again but that man… that stupid idiot man.

'I wish you wouldn't smoke, dear. What if someone sees?'

'It's your fault I'm here at all.'

'The little children, dearest, they look up to me; to *us*.'

She chanced a glance at Santa. His brilliant red jacket was now a patchwork of soot stains and there was a fresh tear in the shoulder.

'Yeah.' Karen grunted, stealing one last drag before stamping the cigarette underfoot. 'Well. Can I go now?'

'Ah, well, I wonder...'

'What?' Karen grunted.

'It's just the old knee, my dear. Dr. Jones said I should rest it but when you pulled me out–'

'I told you not to use the chimneys this year!' Karen snapped. 'I don't know why I waste my breath talking to you.'

'I've only got Glasgow and Falkirk to go, you'll be home in an hour.'

'Am I just free labour to you, is that why you married me? Dragging me out of bed on Christmas Eve–'

'Please Karen, it's for the children. They'll be so disappointed on Christmas morning if Santa hasn't been.' He implored.

'Like I've been every Christmas I've had since I met you.' She muttered, trying to seem indifferent to what the children wanted.

Santa didn't say anything, but she could see he was hurt.

'Fine, whatever.' She huffed, climbing into his sleigh and taking the reins. 'Are you able to get home in my sleigh okay?'

'I'll manage.' He said.

'Well mind and call if you can't–'

'I'll be fine. See you when you get back.'

'Please yourself.' Karen snapped and with a sharp crack on the reigns she took off into the snowy night sky.

Karen muttered profanities to herself as she stuffed yet another oversized stocking (this one belonging to someone called Adam Forrester) with gifts and chocolates.

That man! This was what her life had become. Stockings, presents, Christmas trees and clambering up and down chimneys. It was all he cared about.

Exhausted from her work, she sat down on a nearby armchair. A plastic, cartoon portrait of her good-for-nothing husband grinned back at her from the opposite wall. On the coffee table, a small plate of mince pies sat beside a raw carrot and a glass of milk. Karen shuddered. How long had it been sitting there?

She looked at the clock on the mantle. Half past four. Enough time for a quick one.

Rummaging around in her pocket, she pulled out her cigarettes and lit one, trying to relax on the unfamiliar armchair, taking the mince pies off the plate and lifting the plate onto her lap to use as an ashtray.

Seventeen years of her life she'd wasted, married to a man who cared more about other people's children than about her and about *their* children, not that they had any. He'd swept her off her feet that fateful morning seventeen years ago, when she interrupted him filling her stocking. He whisked her away for a midnight journey around the world in his sleigh and she helped deliver presents to all the children in the world. Afterwards they returned to her place and shared a mince pie before he suddenly announced the sun was rising and he had to leave.

She couldn't let him. She was young, starstruck and there was such an obvious and irresistible chemistry between them that she went with him. She married him and, for a while, life was one big festive adventure but now... now she was trapped in the dwindling hours of an everlasting Christmas evening, when the presents are all unwrapped and the turkey is all gone and the tree doesn't seem to sparkle quite as brightly as it did a few hours before. That was her life, all year round with him locked up in his workshop most of the year then expecting everyone to jump to his command come December. The sleigh was just a mode of transport now. Giving gifts to other people's children was nice but it wasn't quite enough and whenever she tried to talk about starting their own family, he would find some excuse to change the subject or–

'Who are you?'

Karen nearly fell off the armchair as she smashed the cigarette furiously into the plate. There was a man in the doorway, presumably Adam Forrester. He was a little younger than Karen, perhaps, but not by much, maybe early thirties. He didn't look particularly bothered to find a stranger in his living room.

*Of course not. He was expecting one.*

'The first openly female Santa.' Karen grunted.

'Are you Mrs. Claus?'

'Karen.' She grunted. 'Karen Claus. You're supposed to be sleeping.'

'Couldn't sleep.' Adam said, matter-of-factly. 'Too excited. I love Christmas.'

Karen snorted. 'You're worse than my husband.'

'Don't you like Christmas?'

'Every day is Christmas with us.' Karen snorted. 'This is just work. *His* work. Only reason I'm here is he got stuck in a chimney earlier and hurt himself.'

'Oh, so you get lumbered with it whenever he's not well?'

'I don't mind *doing* it.' Karen said. 'It's great giving gifts to all the children and everything, it's just...' Karen paused, hunting for the right word.

'Christmas isn't Christmas any more.' Adam finished for her. 'Like you said, it's work. *His* work.'

'Yeah. Exactly.'

'You wanna talk about it? I know we don't know each other but if you want to let off steam or...'

Karen sighed. 'That's very kind but there's nothing to tell. I'll tell you this though, one day you're gonna meet someone and you'll think to yourself, "that's it, *this* is the One for me!", 'cause there's so much chemistry between you and you think he'll make all your wildest dreams come true. But you can't live like that...' Karen looked in her cigarette box. It was empty. 'You marry someone like that and you realise what's really important to you. Not the sleigh rides or the presents or the fact he can do magic. Boring stuff, like raising a family and knowing he cares about you more than all that other stuff; Christmas, or whatever it is makes him feel good about himself.'

'I guess being married to Santa must be a bit like being married to a celebrity.' Adam mused. 'Christmas is what he is and everyone loves him for it, expects it from him. And you just get absorbed into all that whether you like it or not.'

'Yeah.' Karen said. 'Yeah, exactly. So now it's all just Christmas this, Christmas that, all year round. It's not magical any more, but it's not quite a proper life either. And that's what I want, a proper life. I love Santa but I want a normal life too. I want to get excited about Christmas like a normal person and and see my own children getting excited about it every year instead of just standing in the background making Christmas fun for strangers

'You know, we had this big fight last Christmas. Something that was important to me but he didn't want to know. After that he spent all year locked up in his workshop, hardly came out at all, just says he's gotta get ready for Christmas.'

Karen exhaled sharply through her nose. She looked down at her hands and tugged at the fingers of her gloves.

'You know what? No, I don't like Christmas, not any more.'

Adam didn't say anything. She looked up to see him, focusing intently on her with genuine concern on his face. He seemed like a kind man.

'Look, never mind about me.' Karen said, rising to her feet slightly embarrassed by her own catharsis. 'Tell you what, since you love Christmas so much, why don't I give you a quick ride in the sleigh? Just to say thank you.'

Adam's eyes lit up. 'Really? Well… yes! Oh, I'd love that.'

Karen smiled, feeling a whole lot lighter than she did half an hour ago. 'Get your coat. It's chilly out.'

The sleigh ride did not last long. It was too close to daybreak to take Adam beyond his own city. There was a tiny chink of light on the farthest point of the horizon when Karen and Adam landed back on Adam's rooftop and Karen couldn't help feeling disappointed it was over.

'Well,' Adam said without rising up from the sleigh. 'Thanks for a wonderful night.'

'No, thank you for listening to me. For understanding.' Karen said.

Adam smiled and Karen felt her heart skip a beat.

'Well,' She said, business-like. 'You'd better get to bed or Santa won't come.'

Adam took a long time to clamber out of the sleigh. When he finally did get out, he walked around the sleigh to be as close to her as possible.

'You want to come in for a coffee or something?' He asked.

*Yes. Yes, I do.*

'I can't, Adam.' She said, feeling sick. 'The sun's coming up, I have to get back.'

'Before you turn into a pumpkin?'

'Something like that.' She grimaced.

'Alright.' He said, taking a single, very small step back from the sleigh.

'Goodnight, Adam.' She said, cracking the reigns hard to return to Santa.

The sun was just beginning to rise over the snowy Korvatunturian landscape when Karen landed the sleigh in front of the quaint log cabin which was their private residence. Smoke puffed happily from the chimney and a warm glow from the windows gently illumined the snowy ground but she felt more miserable than ever. Two serious faced elves met the sleigh as soon as she arrived, taking charge of the reindeer, allowing her to go immediately to the house.

Inside it was quiet, though the hallway was warm. He was up, but she just wanted to go to bed and forget about the last twenty-four hours.

'Is that you dearest?'

Karen swore under he breath.

'I'm going to bed.' She called back.

'But it's Christmas!' He called back. Karen heard his heavy footfalls coming towards the hall. A moment later, he appeared in the living room door, wearing those ridiculous red and white pyjamas. 'Maybe Santa's been!'

'I live with Santa. It's nothing new.' She grunted, walking past him to the stairs but he gently took her hand and stopped her.

'Karen, please.' He said in a softer voice. 'Come and see.'

'Can I have a fag?'

Santa winced.

'Fine.' Karen sighed. 'But then I'm going to bed.'

Santa stepped back from the living room door, making a grand gesture of inviting her into the room. 'Of course.' He said solemnly.

Karen entered the living room, a little surprised and even a touch disappointed to find it unchanged. Warm, cosy, with a fire blazing in the hearth and the same small bundle of presents under the oversized Christmas tree. Instead of going to the presents, however, Santa crossed the living room towards his workshop and stood beside the door.

'In here.' He said, gesturing to the closed door. 'Merry Christmas.'

Karen regarded him suspiciously and felt an unwanted smile begin to force itself upon the corners of her mouth. 'What is it?' She asked, as disdainfully as she could.

'Your main present,' he said. 'From your husband.'

Karen approached the workshop and pushed the door open. She seldom ventured here herself. It was always full of mess and business as Santa and his elves worked furiously preparing all the toys and gifts for the following Christmas. Something she had lost all interest in.

She could hardly believe her eyes when she

opened the door. All of the workbenches, machinery and magical paraphernalia were gone. There were no elves and no mess. The entire room had been redecorated from top to bottom in soft pastel shades. On one side of the room, there was a white chest of drawers with soft edges and bulbous, rubbery handles. A similarly styled wardrobe stood directly beside it. There was a large selection of soft toys populating the top of the drawers. The windows were covered with pastel blue blackout curtains which prevented any sunlight from getting into the room. There was a white lampshade with tiny little reindeer dangling from the light, casting reindeer shaped shadows all around the room. On the far side of the room, there was a simple white wooden cot and a baby changing station. Karen was speechless.

'Like it?'

'Where's the workshop?' Karen gasped.

'Dismantled.' Santa said. 'I've decided to advertise for someone else to take over. They can have it all. I thought about what you said last Christmas and you were right.'

Karen looked up at her husband, his face uncharacteristically serious though not stern.

'I've been too absorbed in my work. I've just been doing it so long, it's become my life. So it's time to retire. To focus on our family.' He nodded into the workshop-turned-nursery. 'I know this doesn't make up for everything but-'

'But it's a start.' Karen said, nodding. 'And I'm

sorry. For everything.'

'So…' Santa said. 'Not a disappointing Christmas *this* year, then?'

'No.' She said. 'I think this is going to be the best Christmas ever.'

# 6 SIX WORD STORIES (VOL. 1)

*First published various dates*

FAULTY HAT COMMENCES 823bn RABBIT APOCALYPSE.

'Butler dunnit,' written in Butler's blood.

Sword drawn, Julius crossed the Rubicon.

Forsaking arms, we agreed to disagree.

Found the weapon inside the book.

Remembered iPhone; wish I'd remembered iToilet-Roll!

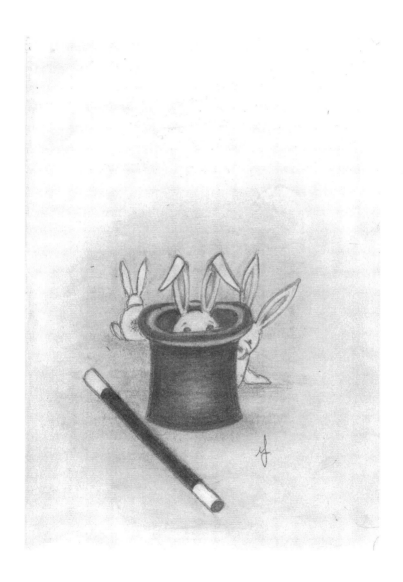

# POPPING OFF

*First published 11th February 2018*

My family have a curse. One hour before death, we become omniscient. Foreknowledge, insight, everything. Can you imagine?

I'm at the office and it's happening to me now. I'm only thirty-one.

Imagine *that*.

I should phone Janice, but when I think how she badgered dad with questions at his Hour...

Stuff it. I'll write her. Might as well use up the office stationary.

'Jan,
*Saturday's lotto numbers: 4, 7, 12, 22, 34, 36, 5.*
*You're welcome.*
*Nick'*

I need to post this quick. I'll be out of time soon.

'Kate, family emergency.' I call to my supervisor. 'Can I pop off early?'

# THE CHURCH
# MOUSE

*First published 7th May 2017*

Based on a true story

[1]

**T**he Landlord and Landlady were busy today, pulling out the furniture and hoovering behind every nook and cranny where I'd been, or even might've been. They even shoved their infernal vacuum nozzle into my room. I wasn't in at the time, praise God. I was out scavenging, but they've definitely been here. They've cleaned up all my business, sure, the bits they could reach anyhow. They've settled down now. Their telly's been on for hours.

Ah, that's it off now. Finally. They'll be going to bed soon, I can hear them moving about. He's washing the dishes, like he usually does just before bed. She'll be upstairs already then. I'll give them an hour, once I'm sure they're asleep and then I'll–

Wait. *Sniffffffff*. What's *that?!*

*Sniff, sniff?*

Chocolate and.. *sniff?...* raisins and *caramel* by goodness! Ohh, mamma mia... *sniffffffff!* Oh yes! A Cadbury's Picnic if I'm not very much mistaken! Ohh, yes, yes, yes, yes, yes, *yes!* I'm eating well tonight!

No! No... no, no, I mustn't yet, he's still out there... gotta wait... gaagh! Hurry up and *leave*, already!

I think... yes, he's gone. I can hear him on the stairs. I should wait but... oooh, I have to have that Picnic! Maybe, I'll just have a peak... he won't be back now till morning anyway... and that smell, it's so strong... it must be...

Yes! There it is, right outside my door! That idiot's left a whole chunk of the stuff just lying around in this little plastic box for me. I'll just pop in, grab the choccie and...

*Ow!* The door just fell on me! It's not very heavy, though, that's something. If I just back-peddle like this I can pull out the choccie and... yes! I'm free! Haha! Oooh, my precious little Picnic, I can't wait to get you back to my room... ! Hehehe!

# [2]

Ooh! Another day, another Picnic! Maybe I've got the Landlord and Landlady all wrong. Maybe they really like me and want me to stay? Eh? Nah, don't be silly. I've had all night to think about this and I don't think that door closed on me accidentally last night! It's just dumb luck, really, that my bum was still hanging out the back or who knows what might've happened...

I should leave it, I know. I've still got plenty left over from last night but... ooooooh, that smell just drives me wild! I got out okay last night, I'll probably be okay again just as long as I'm careful. I know it can be done and... oh mercy, I won't be able to think straight with that sitting outside my front door all night long.

Just need to watch. Make sure, take care, always beware. Don't let them outsmart you. You can do this, just... take care. Beware. Don't let carnal passions cloud your judgement. Use your brain, take your time, claim the prize.

Good... good, it's the same kind of trap as before. Nothing that's gonna snap my back or open my skull. I'll just do what I did last night, leave my bum in the doorway and... gagh, the choccie's a bit smaller tonight though... tucked right away up at the back it is, I can't quite reach... ooooh, but it's right *there,* I can almost taste it! Just another half inch...

Woosh! Rats, rats, ratty-rats! The door's closed!

Ohh, no, no, no, no, no, no, please God, let me out! Let me out! Ooh, God forgive me, I know it's my fault, I... I got greedy and I'm sorry! Please, God, let me out! Please... I'm sorry, I'm sorry... *please!*

[3]

Ngh! What? I must've fallen asleep. But it wasn't a dream. I'm still here, in the stupid box with the stupid choccie. I don't fancy it quite the same any more. I feel sick. I can't move. They're here. The Landlady, she sees me. She's calling to her husband. They're so... *big!*

Aaaagh! He's picking up the box! What's he doing with me? Where's he taking me? To eat me? I hear humans burn up smaller animals before they eat them! Maybe he'll leave me if I just sit very still but... oh no, it's a forlorn hope! What else can I do?

Please, please, please, *please,* Lord God Almighty, rescue me from the hand of this monster! I know it's my fault, I promise I won't ever be greedy again I'll... oh, Lord, please have mercy on me a sinner!

Agh! The light! He's taking me outdoors, into their car... where are we going?

I wish I could move. I'm so afraid, every part of my body feels like it's turned to stone. All except my bowels; they're working overtime. Whatever he's doing, oh Lord, let it be over soon. To die in terror, trapped in this dungeon, tiny even by my standards and drowning in my own business...

He's stopped the car.

Oh… rats.

This is it.

Here it comes. He's picking me up and taking me outside and opening the box… he's shaking it at the ground. In one sudden motion my petrified body and the choccie fall to the ground and land among the long grass on the roadside. I'm out! I'm free! I'm out of here! Oh thank you, thank you, thank you, God! Thank you kind Landlord! I'm free!

*Mr. Mouse fled through the grass and the bushes for hours. He swore never to succumb to gluttony again.*

*In the winter of 2017 he became a church mouse. He devoted his life to the ministry and service of the church and was ordained as a minister in 2018.*

*He died peacefully at the age of three in 2019 and was buried on the grounds of his parish along with the piece of Picnic which he had preserved as a memento of the day his life was spared.*

# 6 SIX WORD STORIES (VOL. 2)

*First published various dates*

KING FELIX DEAD: Nine assassins executed.

My treasure? Buried by my ex.

Took the bait. *Snap!* Hard cheese…

While others cooled, our house burned.

Nine parachutes; ten passengers casting lots.

Turned up volume: '……will self-destruct.'

# LITTLE THIEVES ARE HANGED

*First published 22nd October 2017*

The junkie was talking before he reached the bus stop. Coming toe-to-toe with another gentleman who was waiting there, the junkie recounted his entire life story, occasionally tapping the gentleman's stomach; a genial 'wait-until-you-hear-this' gesture.

The gentleman put his hands in his pockets. He glanced desperately towards me. I smiled, trying to reassure him.

An eternity passed before a bus finally spirited the junkie away, still talking as he embarked. The gentleman relaxed.

'I've no idea who that was!' He confided to me as my bus arrived.

I laughed and boarded the bus, fingering his wallet, safe in my pocket.

# THE FIREPLACE COPPERS

*First published 7th November 2015*

Instead of a fire, my great uncle Carmichael used to keep an enormous glass bottle filled with coppers in the centre of his fireplace. It did nothing to warm the living room, which was always too cold, but instead radiated a subtle blend of Old and Stuffy all around the room.

'How many?' He would grunt, gesturing towards it with his stick whenever I visited with my parents.

*Nine hundred billion! Eleven! Seventy-four thousand and twelve!*

I was so consumed with guessing that I never realised that he didn't know himself. It was only there to break the ice.

# 6 SIX WORD STORIES (VOL. 3)

*First published various dates*                    .

Remembered and avenged every unicycle 'performance.'

Defecated. Swam. 'Oh look, a morsel... '

Murdered thousands for the 'common good.'

Money. Sex. Power. Three wasted wishes.

Ignored camel's nose. Tent crashed down.

New Earth colony. Same old stories.

# SANTA: ORIGINS

*First published 24th December 2017*

'Daddy,' my daughter ventured in the dwindling hours of one Christmas Eve. 'My teacher says Santa's not Santa but St. Nicholas was Santa. And he's dead. So… if Santa is St. Nicholas and St. Nicholas is dead, how can is he coming here?'

'Well Christine,' I began, thinking on my feet. 'Your teacher is right that St. Nicholas has been dead for centuries…'

But seeing a wave of disappointment flash across my daughter's face, I knew I couldn't stop there. This girl still believed. I couldn't just snatch it away from her, but would lying to her face be any better?

'But she left out the part about him being cloned.' I added.

She looked at me like I'd grown antlers.

'Cloned?'

'Yeah, cloned. You know, copied. They made a

new Santa out of the old one.' I continued, trying to look cool. I was committed now. 'His remains were exhumed by *really* clever scientists from the future. They used his remains to create this *clone*, intending to send him back to his own time so that he could continue giving gifts to all the children, just like he used to when he was first alive.'

She still looked confused. 'But... how come he's magic and can fly around the world and stuff now?'

'Well it's not *really* magic.' I explained. 'They used something called *cy-ber-net-ic tech-nology* to make him stronger and faster than he was before. It also meant he'd stay alive much, much longer– maybe even forever.'

She still didn't look convinced.

'Why?' She asked.

'Because,' I sighed, as if it were obvious but my mind was racing. 'He's the kindest man in the world! I'm sure your teacher must've explained that he always used to give gifts to poor children, right? Well, now that he's been enhanced with cybernetic technology, he can give gifts to *all* the children in the world in a single night!'

I could've stopped there. I should've stopped there. But it was obvious she still had questions that needed answers and now that I had begun, I found that I couldn't stop.

'The truth is,' I began slowly, hoping I wasn't robbing her of her innocence too young. 'There will be a war in the future. A terrible war between humanity and the machines they've created.'

Her eyes were like baubles.

'The scientists intended to send Santa back in time to begin giving out gifts as soon as they cloned him, but before they could send him back, the Machines kidnapped the cyber-Santa clone and re-programmed him to turn him against his fellow humans.' I continued. 'They gave him even *more* cybernetic enhancements, including terrifying metal claws, and he rode a mechanical monster with horns and a deadly laser beam that shot out from its nose. He slew thousands of human soldiers until his clothes were stained red with the blood of his own kind. Others they captured and turned into cybernetic slaves called Enhanced Living Flesh (or 'ELFs' for short).

'During one particular massacre, he came upon the cowering figures of a couple of refugees– all children, orphans of the war– and he was suddenly overwhelmed with his own natural, God-given human compassion and regained his own mind. He turned against the Machines and after he defeated them, travelled back to his own time, hoping to regain his former life. But the humans of the past could not accept him, and he was forced to retreat to a remote part of the North Pole. Since then has tried to make amends for the atrocity he committed by using his cybernetic enhancements to secretly bring gifts to all the good boys and girls every year.'

She laughed, a nervous laugh. 'If that's true, why's he so *jolly* all the time then? He's always laughing, "ho ho ho."'

'Oh!' I answered without missing a beat. 'That's not laughter. That's his cybernetic vocaliser. It was damaged during the war. Every now and again it gets caught in a loop and sounds like, "ho, ho, ho, ho, ho, ho."'

She didn't look at all pleased to hear that.

'Is he coming here tonight?' She breathed.

'Of course!' I beamed.

'Christine, don't you listen to your father's horrible stories.' My wife chided from behind me. I hadn't even heard her enter the room. She leaned in close to my daughter and whispered. '*He's* really Santa.'

Christine looked relieved, but I felt exposed. Exposed and undermined. A lump rose up somewhere between my chest and my throat, the likes of which I hadn't felt in years. I had to get out of there before my wife or daughter saw how badly I'd been affected. I retreated as quickly as I could to my room and shut the door– and not a moment too soon. I broke down right there on the bedroom floor.

*'Ho. Ho, h'h'ho, ho. Ho. Ho, ho, ho, ho, ho, ho, ho...'*

# THE MARTIAN'S REVENGE

*First published 6th December 2015*

**D**CI Mcleod had never seen anything like it. The chippy's owner lay dead, his head submerged in the fryer. Witnesses claimed they saw a tall green man burst from the chippy carrying armfuls of Mars bars, who fled the scene in a strange car which literally flew into the night.

# 6 SIX WORD STORIES (VOL. 4)

*First published various dates*

Mushroom cloud, nuclear winter, the end.

*'Sorry I missed you.
– The Cat'*

The Englishman's mortgage was his castle.

Slew the sheriff, saved the maiden.

Mad axe murderer exonerated post execution

Final upstairs climb, borne by ambulancemen.

# THE SECRET OF SIG. PIERONI'S PIZZA

*First published 3rd December 2017*

‘**W**hat if we're caught?' Derek whispered.

'It's *our* customers Pieroni's stealing with his "piping hot pizza delivered in under five minutes."' Sandra hissed. The lock gave. They were in. 'No way he's doing that single-handed, whatever he says. It's a tax thing, gotta be. Try find his ledger.'

'What's this?' Derek whispered, fiddling with an unlabelled control panel beside the pantry. Something inside the pantry began to hum. Derek stepped inside.

'Found it!' Sandra called. 'Let's go!'

No reply.

'Derek!' She whispered, following him into the pantry. 'Quickl-'

They were outdoors.

In the distance, herds of dinosaurs fled an erupting volcano.

# I NEED A HERO

*First published 1st May 2016*

'**G**ood afternoon, you are through to the Free National Heroes Service. My name is Colin, how may I help you?'

*'Yes, good morning, I'd like to book a knight please, for three o'clock tomorrow.'*

'Oook, if you just give me a minute I'll take some details off you...'

*'OK.'*

'Now you do understand I can't guarantee it'll be a knight because—'

*'Why not?'*

'Well you see—'

*'It really needs to be a knight, I always get one. If you check your records you'll see, I always get a knight.'*

'Oook... well, let me just take your details then and I'll have a look for you, OK? What's your name please?'

*'Shona Forrester.'*

'And your date of birth?'

*'Age of Esfin, 03, 36.'*

'Aaaand your address?'

*'0/1 1236 Esclimber Way.'*

'That's great, thanks. Oook, you don't seeeeem to be registered on our system just now but that's OK, I'll just add you on—'

*'Sorry, what do you mean I'm not registered? I've had heroes out here loads of times and I've always got a knight. It's never been a problem before. Has it all changed now?'*

'No, madam, as I tried to explain before, we've only ever had three categories of hero available. You can have a warrior, a mage or a ranger. And you're definitely not on our system either, but that's no problem, I've just added you on now.'

*'Oh! So I can't have a knight then?'*

'I'm afraid it's out of my hands madam, the best I can do is put you down for a warrior and I'll put it in your notes that you wanted a knight. That way Control will see that on their screens when they come to allocate heroes and will do what they can to accommodate you.'

*'So I should still get a knight then?'*

'I really wouldn't like to make any promises, madam, but the Controllers will do their very best if there's one available. You will definitely be able to get a warrior but that's all I can say for certain until you're assigned a hero in the morning.'

*'It's never been a problem getting a knight before but right, whatever... well, OK. Can I go now?'*

'Nooo, not quite yet, I still need to take a few details off you first if you don't mind. Now was it AM or PM tomorrow you wanted this for?'

*'PM, three o'clock please.'*

'OK, now because we've only got so many warriors on at one time, I obviously can't give you a cast iron guarantee that it'll be exactly three o'clock. It just depends what's available. Normally what we'd do is book you in for an AM or PM slot just now and you'll be assigned a time by the Controllers depending on when there's a warrior available. So I'll put you down for PM and put it in your notes that you'd prefer it for three, is that OK?'

*'Well what time is he likely to arrive then?'*

'I honestly couldn't say for sure, madam, that's entirely down to Control, I'm afraid. An afternoon booking could be any time between twelve o'clock and half eight.'

*'OK, make it AM then.'*

'Are you sure that's OK? That would be any time then between nine o'clock and twelve.'

*'It'll have to be, it's no use him coming at all if he's any later than three, half three at the latest, so I'll go with AM. Can you let me know roughly what time that's likely to be? I'll be at work in the morning so I'll need to ask my neighbour to let him in.'*

'Like I already said madam, I've no way of knowing until you've been allocated a hero what time it'll be, except that it'll be in the morning between nine and twelve. I can get Control to give you a call once you've been allocated if you like?'

'Fine, thank you.'

'No problem, now I just need to check your eligibility to use this service—'

*'Why do you need to do that? I've had heroes out before, loads of times.'*

'I'm sorry madam, but there was definitely nothing at all on our system for you. Are you sure you didn't use a private guild last time?'

*'No, I've always dialled this number. There must be something wrong with your system.'*

'Mmm, maybe but I need to check your eligibility anyway or my system won't let me make the booking. Is that OK?'

*'How long do you think he'll be anyway? I mean, I need to know when he'll be back from his quest so I can make sure there's someone in. I'll be at work till two.'*

'Well, that really depends. I was actually just about to ask you exactly why you need a hero. I mean, is there any one else who can go for you?'

*'What difference does that make?'*

'Well, you see even though this as a free service, we don't receive any government or lottery funding so it's really only those who are completely unable to go on the quests themselves that we can provide this service for.'

*'Bu—!'*

'And there's no way I could guess at how long your hero will take to complete his quest unless I know what it is. Also Control need to know in advance if he needs any special equipment; things like enchanted armour or really bulky things like rune stones or armoured horses might take a bit longer to arrange.'

*'Well, he won't need any of that so there's no problem.'*

'I'm sure there isn't, but I need to ask you what his quest will be anyway or I can't take your booking.'

*'I just need him to go to the supermarket for me. I need him to pick up some things for my son's birthday and I can't go 'cause I've got work!'*

'The supermarket?'

*'Yes. It's never been a problem before today!'*

'I'm really sorry, you'll need to go with a private guild for something like that.'

*'But—!'*

'I am really sorry, but there's nothing I can do. This is a free service and we don't receive any government or lottery funding so we really can only provide this service for extremely dangerous or difficult quests and to those with a household income of less than twelve-thousand *quil* per year. Is there anything else I can help you with today?'

*'…'*

*Click.*

'Bye then.' *Click.* 'Geeeeeez… Unbelievable!'

'Let me guess,' said Colin's supervisor. 'It's young master Forrester's birthday again?'

'Yeah!'

'Hmph! That'll be his fifth birthday this year then!'

# 6 SIX WORD STORIES (VOL. 5)

*First published various dates*

Rose wrote to Henry: 'Dear John…'

Downloaded *Treasure Island* for free.
…
… … What?

Caught the lifebuoy. Saved the dog.

Removed the prickles. Lost the cactus.

Reading 'Final Demand', eating final breakfast.

Halloween: masked thief escaped into crowd.

# COLD BRASS

*First published 20th December 2015*

The trumpet's mouthpiece was as cold as ice on my lips but the supermarket's manager had promised the band free mince pies if we stood out in the snow and played a few carols to the shoppers.

Easy.

Now if only I could get this thing off my face…

# THE MONSTER

*First published 27th August 2017*

C aptain Harold of Earth's Space Navy had met his share of bizarre alien cultures, but nothing like these. These were monsters.

One of the Creatures stood over Harold, injecting him with chemicals and mutilating him with ferocious tools. The Creature had cold blue hands, shining black eyes and no mouth (yet it spoke). A human female observed nearby, desensitised to the atrocity she was witnessing.

The Creature stepped back.

'There, that wasn't so bad,' it smiled.

'What do you say to the dentist, Harry?' the human (code name: MUM) goaded.

They had practised this before they left the house. *Thank you Mr. Riley.* Harold's mouth was still numb but he had to try…

'Yeou're a monsther!' he screamed.

# 6 SIX WORD STORIES (VOL. 6)

*First published various dates*

BEETHOVEN CLONE DEMANDS ROYALTIES BACK PAY.

CLONE LAB ARSON ATTACK: NO SURVIVORS.

MARTIANS: No spacesuits on the beach!

Beautiful dress, perfect make-up, impure intentions

Lost a bet– and my taste-buds!

Wished for love. Got a dog.

# THE GIRL & THE CAR

*First published 27th May 2018*

The car was mine. I found it, so it was mine.

I don't know how it got there. I was just playing in the bushes at the bottom of the hill one day and there it was, in the clearing. It didn't have any glass in the windows and two of the doors were missing. Also the steering wheel came off if you turned it too hard.

I couldn't have been happier. My own car. A real one. I let Michael and Paul use it too, and sometimes I even let them drive it because it's no fun on your own. That was okay because they knew it was mine because I found it. I didn't tell Mum and Dad about it and I told Paul and Michael not to tell their mums and dads either. Adults have funny ideas about things like that. I knew they wouldn't let me keep the car, even though I found it fair and square and it didn't really go.

It was Sunday. Me and Michael were playing Batman in the car while we waited for Paul. His family went to a different church from me and Michael so we always met him after lunch. I was Batman (obviously, because it was my car) but it was Robin's turn to drive.

When Paul arrived, he had a girl with him.

'Girls aren't allowed in the car!' Michael objected. 'Why'd you even bring her here? This is private property.'

'Aw, c'mon Mikey, she's my cousin!' Paul whined. 'Mum said I had to. It's just for today. I swear I tried not to but they said I had to or I couldn't come out. I swear I tried!'

'Well, she'll have to sit in the back!' I decreed, thinking myself generous. I don't know how old she was but she was younger than us. Too young. And a girl.

'I want to drive!' She cried with glee. 'Please please please please, pretty, pretty please!'

'No.' I said. Enough was enough.

'How not?'

''Cause. It's my car. Girls aren't allowed.'

'Come on, Haitch, let her have a go.' Paul said. 'It's only for today.'

'He's siding with her!' Michael jeered, gripping the wheel even though it had fallen off again.

'I'm not! It's just Mum said I had to or I couldn't come out. It's only for today. Come on!'

'Your mum only said she had to come with you.

She's with you.' I ruled. 'She doesn't even know about the car so that doesn't count.'

'Henry!' Michael hissed, grabbing my arm. 'What if she tells?'

'I'm telling!' The girl taunted us. 'I'm telling, I'm telling!'

'That was your fault!' I said, punching Michael in the arm.

'How's it my fault? Paul brought her!' He hit me back, though not hard. I guess he knew it was his fault.

'I'm telling, I'm telling!' The girl sang in words that didn't rhyme. 'Let me drive or I'm telling!'

'Henry, just let her drive!' Paul pleaded. 'What's the big deal? It's only for one day.'

'She's a girl!' I exploded. 'And she's too wee, she'll tell!'

'I'll not tell if you let me have a go.' She promised. I was about to argue but–

'Alright.' Michael said, opening the imaginary door and climbing out. 'You can have a go, just a quick one mind! But you'd better not tell!'

Treachery!

'That's not how it works!' I said, clambering across to the driver's seat and grabbing the wheel. 'It's mine!' I said, pointing to the place on the dash where I had scratched 'HBS' into the dashboard. That's my initials: Henry Barrington-Smyth. 'I found it, so it's mine!'

'Fine!' The girl shouted. 'It's a stupid car anyway! I've got a better one at my bit, with proper doors and windows and everything! And it drives for real! And you're not getting a go!'

Then she went away. Paul went after her.

'Just let her go!' I shouted after him. He turned to face us but kept walking backwards slowly.

'I can't! My mum, she said…' He trailed off. Then he turned and ran after her.

'Paul! Paul! Just let her go, Paul!'

He ignored me. Michael ran after him, leaving me alone in the car. I couldn't move. It felt important to hold my ground in the car. The car was mine as long as my bottom was on the seat and my hands were on the wheel. Ahead, at the edge of the clearing, I saw Michael grab Paul by the arm to pull him back. Paul shrugged him off and shouted something at him. I don't know what it was but his face was livid. He stormed off through the bushes, out of the clearing. Michael followed him, shouting after him but was back a few moments later. He came back to the car.

'Henry, what if she tells?' Michael asked again. His voice was quivering and his face was ashen.

'She won't tell.' I said, fighting to ignore a hollow sensation in my stomach. 'Paul won't let her. She won't tell. She was just saying that.'

Well, she told. Ten minutes later, Michael's mum came down into our clearing where our car was parked. We were still sitting there, forcing ourselves to be Batman and Robin. Michael got such a blazing row off his mum that I didn't know where to look. She gave me a good tongue lashing as well, then I went home and got more of the same from my own mum. I wasn't surprised by that. Once one adult knows something, they all know it.

We never saw Paul for weeks after that. He didn't go to the same school as me and Michael and whenever we went in for him, we were told he couldn't come out. I felt sick. What if he wasn't talking to us any more, all because of some stupid burnt out car? Michael and me never spoke about it but I think he felt the same. Then one day Paul came in for me. Turned out his parents had just grounded him and never told us, not even when we went in for him.

We never saw the car again. In some ways, it was a relief. We went back to the clearing a while later (and I mean a long while later) but the car was gone. I don't know where. We didn't dare ask. It didn't matter that it had my initials on it or that I found it. It wasn't mine any more. I don't think it ever had been.

Printed in Great Britain
by Amazon